Chocolate Milk

By: Alexandria Rizik

Illustrated By: Joey A Dimaguila

ISBN: 0-9988416-1-7
ISBN-13: 978-0-9988416-1-8

Alexandria's Dedication:

This book is for all of the "different" people in the world — the rare and special gems that aren't afraid to be themselves. We all have unique characteristics that separate us from others. Be yourself and embrace your oddities.

Also, thank you to my parents who raised me to follow my dreams and to never care what others think.

Joey Dimaguila would like to thank:

My wife May, and children Jen, Jhasmine, John Mark, Jem and Joana

Mr. Jones just delivered the last baby cow. He could tell that this cow was special.

He decided to name her Star because she had a star-shaped spot on the side of her back.

Months had passed since the delivery and all of the cows were about to be milked for the first time.

Mr. Jones started with Penelope. Perfect, white milk filled the bucket.

Next was Emerald. She also produced perfect, white milk.

Finally, it was Star's turn.

When Mr. Jones began to milk her, he realized that her milk was coming out brown.

"Ew!" cried Penelope.

"Gross! Her milk is brown!" added Emerald.

"Girls, be nice to your sister. She can't help what color her milk is." Mr. Jones defended Star.

Either way, the hurtful comments really upset her.

She frowned and walked away to her own corner of the farm.

10

Mr. Jones decided to call the doctor right away.

The doctor didn't know what to make of this situation.

After giving Star a full checkup, he tasted the brown milk. A smile spread across his face from ear to ear.

"This is delicious. It's chocolate!"

Mr. Jones' jaw dropped. "Chocolate? Let me try!"

Mr. Jones took a sip of the chocolate milk.

"Holy cow!" Mr. Jones exclaimed.

Star smiled. She was glad to see that her milk had pleased the two men.

"You should sell this, Mr. Jones," said the doctor.

14

After the doctor left, Mr. Jones got right to work. He milked Star for three hours straight and then packaged the milk in bottles.

He took it to the farmer's market the next morning.

15

People were hesitant to try the milk because of its brown coloring.

"Ew! It's brown!" cried a child.

"Try it," Mr. Jones said.

16

The child sniffed the bottle before taking a tiny sip. His face lit up with a huge smile.

"This is amazing!" he cheered as he walked over to Star, petting her back. She smiled.

"Let me try," his father asked.

Mr. Jones handed him a bottle. He also took a small sip.

"It's delightful!"

He chugged down the rest of the chocolate milk.

"I'll have another bottle, Mr. Jones," the father said as he finished his last sip.

Everyone gathered around, buying gallons of Star's chocolate milk. Mr. Jones sold out within minutes.

"You really are a star, Star!" he said as they walked back to the farm.

One day, while Mr. Jones was milking Star, Penelope and Emerald walked over to him.

"Can we try some?" asked Penelope.

"Of course," answered Mr. Jones. He handed them a bowl of chocolate milk.

Emerald and Penelope each took a taste.

"Mmmmm!" said Emerald.

"It's Mooolicious, Star!" added Penelope.

"Sorry we made fun of you, just because of the color of your milk," they both apologized.

"It's okay. Sometimes appearances can be deceiving!"

THE END

The Author

Alexandria was born and raised in Scottsdale, Arizona. She was brought up by a large Armenian family. Her love for writing began when she was a young child and her aunt bought her a journal. She told Alexandria to write her a story and the rest is history. She received a degree in English from Arizona State University. She enjoys writing Young Adult Fiction along with many other genres of writing; from poetry to children's picture books. Her favorite part about writing is being able to write the "happily ever after" that doesn't always happen in real life.

Alexandria's story, "Chocolate Milk", was originally written for an assignment for her English class when she was 17-years-old while she was simultaneously running an anti-bullying campaign. She wanted to share this message of why it is wrong to judge others with the world.

The Illustrator

Joey Dimaguila started drawing at an early age in his native hometown in Tipas, Taguig City, Philippines.

Born to a family of artists and musicians, Joey has a passion for both conservative and contemporary Arts, loves the music of the Beatles, Dave Clark Five, England Dan and John Ford Coley, Kalapana and the Eagles among others.

Joey draws inspiration from his wife May, his children, friends, officemates at the City Engineers Office, PBID, Manila, where he is currently working as an Artist Illustrator.

Made in the USA
Middletown, DE
20 September 2023

38807453R20015